HORROR STORIES
TO TELL IN THE DARK

BOOK 4

SHORT SCARY ANTHOLOGY STORIES FOR
TEENAGERS AND YOUNG ADULTS

BRYCE NEALHAM

HORROR STORIES TO TELL IN THE DARK: BOOK 4

Copyright © by Bryce Nealham.

All rights reserved. No part of this publication may be reproduced, distributed, or transmitted in any form or by any means, including photocopying, recording, or other electronic or mechanical methods, or by any information storage and retrieval system without the prior written permission of the publisher, except in the case of very brief quotations embodied in critical reviews and certain other noncommercial uses permitted by copyright law.

This is a work of fiction. Names, characters, business, events and incidents are the products of the author's imagination. Any resemblance to actual persons, living or dead, or actual events is purely coincidental.

HORROR STORIES TO TELL IN THE DARK: BOOK 4

CONTENTS

WICKED GAMES 1
    A. M. Axinte 9
THE LAST ONE 11
    Britney Supernault 21
DON'T SLEEP! 23
    Frederick Trinidad 35
SINISTER 37
    Chemsou Khodja 45
CARRIED AWAY 47
    Manuel Bocchia 59
BUZZ 61
    Oktay Ibrahimov 69

HORROR STORIES TO TELL IN THE DARK: BOOK 4

Find Out About Our Latest Horror Book Releases...

Simply go to the URL below and you will be notified as soon as a new book has been launched.

bit.ly/3q34yte

"We all go a little mad sometimes."

— Norman Bates – *Psycho (1960)*

"No tears please, it's a waste of good suffering."

— Pinhead – *Hellraiser (1987)*

HORROR STORIES TO TELL IN THE DARK: BOOK 4

WICKED GAMES

By A. M. Axinte

They say that you shouldn't play with people's faith – that fragile thing, which humans are so afraid of – because you don't know what could happen if you tangle the string of their destiny around your filthy fingers.

You could end their happiness, career and even their life with just a snap of their neck... The questions remain, though: would you be strong enough to carry the sins of your odious crimes? Will you be able to sleep at night, knowing that something terrible will happen? That something or someone will come after you, looking for justice?

Most of us wouldn't be able to confront this cruel reality day after day, but Cassian Alarick will look at you with a straight face, not showing any emotion, slowly taking the lit cigarette out of his mouth and blowing the toxic smoke right in your face, before speaking with evidently, annoyance in his voice asking just a banal question: how much?

This man didn't care about destiny, people or God. He was a lawyer! His only job was to help rich, influential and important people escape accusations, sentences or prison these bastards will do, literally, anything for a clean image. Some are deputies, mayors or even part of a dangerous gang, but these things were irrelevant to the man, as long you have enough money, it didn't matter who you are or what you did.

He was known as "the devil's advocate", always against the truth and justice, working in the name of the law for people who deserved to be dead for their infractions. Criminals, psychopaths, mafia's leaders, drug dealers, his list was long, but all these have something in common: money.

There was that old proverb: Money is like seawater. The more you drink, the thirstier you become. And the lawyer was always thirsty for a big amount of dollars and blood…

His past was rough, bloody and solicited hard work to be covered, but now he was a clean man in the eyes of the law. However, society wasn't so fond of him, not after seeing his true face in the court, where he defended those horrible people, so proudly, calm and convincing. The other's opinion didn't matter to the lawyer, because he always won the cases.

But, even this man has an unspoken secret, that follows him every moment he closes his eyes: the salty taste of blood that filled his mouth, the sharp and intoxicating smell of gasoline, a cloudy night, when the moon has only thrown some pale rays from time to time, and an opaque shadow that approached him, trying to get him in its cold embrace.

He never knew, where that memory comes from, or if it is only a nightmare, but the truth is: he was scared, not only about that peculiar shadow but by being captured in the void of it.

It is a cloudy night, where the air is too heavy to breathe and too cold for this time of the year, where the full moon is playing hide-and-seek behind the dark clouds and the silence is the only sound you can hear. And like any other night, Cassian woke up in the cold sweat of the same dream.

He was left without breath with a hand on his chest, trying to slow down his heartbeats and regain himself, meanwhile with the other hand; he was searching the glass of water, which he always leaves on the nightstand. But, something strange did happen! The glass wasn't there! For the first time in 10 years, the man didn't find the glass.

"Searching for this?" A low voice spoke with a sly amusement from the armchair, across the room.

Cassian's heart almost skipped a beat, hearing the cold voice. His wide eyes narrowed in the direction of the armchair, but in the darkness, he could only distinguish the shadow of a man sitting cross-legged holding in his right hand a glass, most probably his glass of water.

"What are you doing here?" Regaining himself, the lawyer spoke with a calm voice, this wasn't the first time, where someone tried to get rid of him. And, surely, wasn't the last...

"Hmm, interesting! You didn't ask for a name or identity. You see, most humans use their first question trying to get a name like you can use that card to save your life. Ha, pathetic!"

The man chuckled dryly at his own words. Meanwhile, the moon offered a few moments of light in the tiny room, but it's only reached the man's knees, keeping his face in the mysterious darkness. At the same time, the lawyer put his hand on the gun, hide under his pillow, a wrong move and the man will be dead.

"I asked you something! What do you want from me?" Cassian started growing more impatient, tightening his grip on the arm

"Oh, I want many things for you, but for now, I will restrain to one: start working for me, from now on. After all, people call you my advocate, or am I wrong?"

The sly smirk that was plastered on his face, the smoothness of his voice and the great confidence he showed, made Cassian tremble a little in fear.

"I have another client before you, but why don't you tell me the details of the case?" The lawyer wasn't a fool, he knew better than anyone that if you decline an offer from someone that broke into your house, you could be left cold on the floor with a slit at your throat.

"Ah, such a pragmatic human, but also stupid like the others! And... about Andrew Ross, haven't you heard? He is dead!"

The surprised look on Cassian's face makes the man in the shadow continues. "Yeah, he was found without breath on the floor, with his eyes wide open and full of pain and fear, quite funny, isn't it?"

The dark humor didn't amuse the lawyer. His, now, dead client, was a famous Army Sniper, with a sense of amusement a bit odd, because he only laughed when he was scared, a smart self-defense mechanism in his opinion. But, the real question was: how did the man, in front of him, know where Andrew was hidden? Nobody, besides him, knew the secret location!

"What are you?" At this point, the lawyer was sure that this mysterious man wasn't a human, not, after so many years working in this field, he recognized the signs left in the way the man spoke and his words: using the term humans for people, breaking into his house, the affirmation about his advocate and even knowing some information that nobody could ever know.

"Wow, you know how to read a person, huh? You're one of the first humans that ask the right question! I know that you don't believe in God, but I can make you believe in me!"

After a short pause, the man spoke again. "Hmm, what if I show you something?"

In the next seconds, with a supernatural speed that left only a shadow behind, the man was in front of him and before Cassian could react, a cold hand wrapped around his neck lifting him from the bed.

"Now... look at me!" The grip slowly started to tighten, so the lawyer looked straight into the eyes of the man in front of him, and a choked scream tried to escape through his parted lips

The person before him wasn't a human at all! A hideous creature was revealed in the white light of the moon, still dressed in a stylish suit, the entire body was emitting a strong power and strange hotness like fire was running through its veins, he felt burned where the creature was holding him by the neck.

Slowly, lifting his eyes, he saw the head... only an ugly skull with sharp teeth contouring a crazy smile, but the most terrifying part of all were its eyes...

Instead of the ocular globes, there were two dark holes with a ball of fire in each of them, looking at Cassian with a piercing stare that reached his heart and bones; he couldn't tear his gaze apart, it was like he was entranced or forced against his will to look deeply into that fire.

The flames slowly played before him and started creating shapes that evolved in blurry images at first, but he recognized them, with an aching pain: of his first case, exactly at the moment where he won in favor of his client: a notorious drunkard, that beaten up his wife for no reason, and the poor woman on the other side of the court screamed in pain, finding out that his husband will be released free.

Without thinking too much he gained enough courage to shoot two bullets right in the creature's chest, where the lawyer hoped to be the heart.

When the hand that was wrapped around his neck started to

loosen, the man thought that everything was over and for a few wonderful seconds, he had a drop of desperate faith, in a dark corner of his cold soul.

But the bullets only tickled the ego of the creature, because he only laughed shadily before saying:

"Poor, stupid human! When will you learn that the Evil can't be murdered by your pathetic toys, that you call arms?"

At the question, he once again started to grow more impatiently, the tone of his voice changed from the calm and silky one to the more angry and grotesque one, his grip tightening around Cassian's neck, till his face became purple in the lack of oxygen and by stopping his blood circulation.

"P-p-please… let m-me b-b-breath…" The lawyer tried to say, lifting his teary eyes to the creature's ones.

And at that moment, the human had an epiphany! Looking into this demon's eyes he saw images, of himself, of his past… of his odious dream, that haunt his sleep every night for the past 10 years!

Slowly, a faint smell of gasoline reached up to his nostrils, besides the smell of something burning, which was a little more prominent in the air that barely got in the lawyer's lungs.

He could feel something warming him up from the feet, and lastly, he caught some noise, almost inaudible ones; but before he could roll his eyes in an almost-dead state, he heard a much-pitched scream coming from behind, he didn't recognize it at first, but he swears on his life! It was a woman, and it was his mom!

"Oh, no, no, no! Don't you dare to leave me alone here; I didn't finish it with you!" The Devil was talking with the almost dead body before changing his mind and speaking again.

"Hmm, actually, I have a better idea, though! Why don't we meet on the other side, huh? But not before I had my fun with your ignorant dream!"

Cassian woke up in his bed, full of sweat and trembling so hard that the water of glass almost slipped from his hand. Gulping all the water so fast he choked and started coughing loud.

It was just a dream. It was just a dream, a terrific nightmare, only a product of my imagination and nothing else! He tried to convince himself with the loud affirmations, but even he knew that it was too real, it felt too real to be only a nightmare!

The lawyer closed his eyes and calmed his heartbeat, after a while, he was slowly driven into sleep, but before he could relax completely, he felt a cold sensation at his feet that started ascending to his knees and his stomach, before stopping there.

With his eyes wide open, Cassian gulped, and with trembling fingers, he lifted the blanket looking under it and seeing nothing.

He chuckled a little at his craziness and blamed the tiredness for all the, so he covered himself properly and dropped his head on the pillow closing his eyes to sleep well this time. No more dreams, no more nightmares, no more demons with fire in the eyes and no more… smell of gasoline? Wait a minute!

Opening his eyes once again, he saw it! Right above himself, he recognized the shadow that tried to catch him every time in his sleep!

With an ugly shape that changed continuously and expanded more and more, Cassian froze with his gaze on a specific spot… its smile. He could swear, that the shadow never smiled in his dreams, but that horrific grin wasn't a part of it, that devilish smirk was someone else's.

Before he could react in any way the shadow left behind a malefic laugh and threw itself on the man. Without any choice, Cassian let out a powerful scream full of pain and desperation when the, now, creature devoured him piece by piece, splashing the blood everywhere in the room: on the bed, on the floor, on the walls and even on the ceiling.

The man was screaming and crying with such humiliation in front of his death that nobody could save him. With his last powers he screamed only a thing before the monster ripped off his head from the rest of the remaining body:

"I'm so sorry, mom!"

The lawyer wasn't a bad person, in the beginning, he always wanted to make his mom proud and bring her only happiness, but the faith isn't always right, because a drunken man killed his mom, right in front of his eyes.

Nobody believed him, neither the law, neither the lawyers nor even God, so he made an extreme decision: to play dirty from now on! No more honesty, no more kindness and no more forgiveness!

His mother was everything he had, so he will take everything from anybody else!

But... you can't play wicked games with the Devil itself, not when you were serious competition for him.

ABOUT THE AUTHOR

A. M. Axinte

If you need to describe someone, words will never be enough; because you can't really understand somebody, even after a lifetime of knowing them.

I can only use a few words that could evoke my persona: creative, spontaneous and hard-working.

I know, I know, it may sounds a little bit selfish to analyze and give you appreciative pieces of myself; but as much I'd like to aspire, these so said *qualities* may be as well defects!

But, you shouldn't judge a book by its cover, so be kind and take my existence as it is and don't brag about it.

Writing is the destructive passion that burns inside me every day, and as a slave of my mind, I let my soul be consumed by it.

If I should give a little advice, to any reader or writer, I will simply say: be a little mean, or selfish, and think about your happiness.

THE LAST ONE

By Britney Supernault

The computer beeped wildly as Malcolm sat frozen, staring at the screen.

His heartbeat matched the erratic beeps emanating from his computer screen before he laughed loudly.

"I've done it! I've found it!" He shouted as he spun his chair around and stood up with arms raised proudly above his head. Of course, there was no one else left in the room – they had all gone home to their husbands and wives hours ago.

Suddenly the realization of what this meant hit and his blood ran cold as he fell back into his chair.

"I've found the anomaly. The one that they've been hiding..." His heart sped up as perhaps the most important decision of his career, no, his life, stood in front of him.

He swung back around and looked at the data, his glasses reflecting the blue light from the screen as he quickly read exactly what his employer had been hiding.

"Transmissions from the space station...incident with outer

checks...camera images?" Malcolm clicked through to where there was a recording of one of the space station's cameras, pointed toward the outer west wing of the station.

Suddenly a black shadow appeared in the frame.

Malcolm peered closer to the image. It looked to be something on the camera lens. Except it was impossibly fast in zero gravity. And its shape was constantly shifting, like static on an old TV screen.

"What the hell is that?" Malcolm whispered to himself in the empty communications room. His eyes were glued to the screen.

Another figure made an appearance.

An astronaut, making his rounds on the western wing. Malcolm watched as he carried what looked like a utility bag with him. The shadow took on a human figure shape and walked along the outside of the craft.

His fingers felt cold as unease sank his stomach, unable to not watch what he knew was going to happen.

The astronaut contacted the exterior outer wing, connecting to the safety line while the shadow crept closer. A predator to its prey.

"No, look up. Look up dammit. See it." Malcolm urged from his computer screen on Earth, a year later than when the recording happened.

Malcolm gripped the desk as the shadow moved in unexplainable ways. The metal of the exterior bent with every step.

The astronaut looked up and Malcolm could see the fear in his body as he froze and stared.

Before Malcolm could blink, the astronaut was flailing wildly as the shadow disappeared. The struggle went on for about 30 seconds as Malcolm watched in horror. Then the astronaut went limp, his lifeless body floating in the deep darkness of space, still attached to the exterior of the space station.

"What the fu-"

Malcolm jumped back from his desk with fright, startled by the sudden appearance of the shadow standing right in front of the camera. Its silhouette almost blocked the entire view, and Malcolm can see the constant shifting of whatever the hell this shadow was made of.

Malcolm stood still, unmoving from his spot in the dark communications room, staring at the screen.

He knew it was a recording. He knew it was from a year earlier. Yet, the shadow thing was staring at him. He felt goosebumps raise over his body as he stood in this staring competition through time with whatever the hell the shadow was.

Suddenly the recording ended, and the screen exited to a blue screen.

The blue light bounced off Malcolm's open-mouthed face as he finally took a breath.

What the hell was that thing.

Malcolm suddenly understood why his employer, a government-funded space communications base, decided to bury it.

Malcolm also understood how deep of a hole he was in.

It began 10 months ago when they were briefed on a nameless incident that required their astronauts to come back 3 weeks earlier than planned and that they weren't allowed to ask questions.

It didn't make sense.

But now, Malcolm's curiosity had given him the answers he was looking for. But it only led to more confusion.

Malcolm hung up his coat in their hallway closet with a sigh.

He noted that a new jacket had made its appearance. A bright turquoise jacket with gold buttons. His wife had been shopping again, he thought with a chuckle.

"Honey, is this another coat to add to your collection?" He said aloud while loosening his tie.

His wife popped her head around the corner, leaning against the doorway.

"Maybe." She said coyly as she brushed her hands on her apron.

"I thought you hated Turquoise. You said that the color was only for 80's housewives who didn't know how to dress." He teased before kissing his wife.

"What is the saying? Humans can change?" She asked while motioning him towards the table where a freshly cooked meal was awaiting him.

"People, honey, people never change." He said as he sat down.

A flash of something passed Martha's face. But she quickly giggled with a smile before pouring him a glass of brandy.

Martha hadn't always dolled on him like this before. No, when he married her, she had been quite offended with the idea of housewives and women in the kitchen. But about 9 months ago, she had quite the epiphany. Or at least that's what she said when he asked after 3 days straight of cooked meals when he got home. But he wasn't about to complain.

The next day, Malcolm paced back and forth outside the office of his supervisor whom he'd trust with his life, Max Li.

It wouldn't have been Dr. Li who hid the information. No, this was strict classification, meaning it came from the top. But now Malcolm was deciding to bring him into it.

"Sir, you initially hired me because you liked my tenacity and quick wit, correct?" Malcolm started as his boss turned around in his seat from the window facing the base's launchpad.

"Hmmm, let's go with yes..." He said calmly while observing Malcolm, who suddenly felt his tie was too tight.

"Okay, well sir... I've... Well, I've..." He began to sweat under the heavy gaze of his supervisor. His throat felt like it was going to close.

"Well spit it out, Malcolm." Said Dr. Li.

"I've found a recording of human's first contact with an alien life form that our company's been covering up for the past year."

A wide, eerie smile was plastered on Dr. Li's face when Malcolm looked back up. Malcolm backed up instinctively.

"You did, didn't you Malcolm." Was all Dr. Li said, his eyes unblinking.

Malcolm felt ice form in the pit of his stomach as he cleared his throat. There was no going back now.

"Yes, sir. And I don't know what to do with the information. I know -"

"And what do you intend to do with the information, Malcolm?" Dr. Li's face hadn't changed one bit throughout all of Malcolm's rambling. Malcolm felt the hair on his arm and neck raise up.

"Well, there is only one thing we need to do sir. We need to tell the government. They need to know right?"

Something like anger flashed across Dr. Li's face, but his sickly smile stayed on.

"What. A. Shame. Malcolm. We thought you'd be different. A good host body. But if you're only looking to destroy us. Well..." Dr. Li pressed a button underneath his desk and an alarm set off the entire building. The lights flashed off and bright orange lights come on. Malcolm felt something hard knock against his head, and everything went dark.

Malcolm woke up in a cold room. Bright white lights shone down on him as he attempted to move his arms and legs. But they were restrained with hard metal cuffs.

Malcolm yelped as he tried to squeeze his wrist out of the restraints, but it only painfully pulled at his skin. Tears streamed down his face in frustration.

Suddenly another spotlight switched on, lighting up Malcolm even more, but also the room surrounding him. A crowd stood in a circle around him. Their faces were blank and staring.

"Help! Oh God, someone, help me. Dammit!" Malcolm cried as he again tried to pull from the restraints. He nearly ripped his arm out of its socket and his wrists were now beginning to bleed from trying to fit them through the small metal restraints. But no one rushed to help him.

Malcolm cried out and focused his attention on trying to see where he was. A large, metal, smooth structure stood tall behind the large crowd of people.

A rocket.

He was in the launching bay.

His eyes traveled around the large room and with horror he saw bodies hanging from the roof. Limp, and still, faces blank and lifeless, like pieces of meat being cured. Malcolm screamed again.

Where the hell was, he. Why were there people hanging on the ceiling? Hundreds of them.

"Malcolm. We've met before." All the voices rang out in an eerie symphony that echoed in the cavernous launching bay.

"Please, help me..." Malcolm whimpered.

"In the office. In the grocery store. In your favorite pub. Even in your own house, Malcolm." The voices rang out once again, a chorus that struck fear into Malcolm's heart. He began to cry.

"My house? Oh, my wife... Please. I'm married. I won't tell people. I swear. I promise." Malcolm slammed against the restraints, trying to pull both his hands and feet from the restraints. He suddenly felt a comforting hand at his wrist.

He opened his eyes and saw his wife, Martha. A smile on her lips as she peered down at him.

"Martha! Honey! Please. Help me." Malcolm whimpered.

Her eyes were glassy. As she continued to smile complacently at him. Realization dawned on him, and he screamed, spittle flying from his mouth.

"Why would we ever do that Malcolm?" Her voice wasn't her own. It was joined with the sinister symphony of voices.

"God! Why. What the hell did you do. What the hell did you do?"

The voices took a step closer.

"We saw you, Malcolm. Through the camera. And we thought you were the one. The one that could house me for the time being."

Malcolm's mind flashed back to the recording he had seen only last night. How he wished he had just turned off the computer monitor. He cried as they stepped closer and closer, each step in unison, reverberating off the wall.

"But now, Malcolm, now we see that you only have one purpose." Malcolm saw each person push to get closer until they were as close as Martha was.

"What do you want?" Malcolm whispered as his heart thumped madly through his chest.

"The world, Malcolm, the world. I've been hungry Malcolm. But I usually only take one body. But your species is so empty minded," The breathy voice deepened as if it was drawn from the depths of hell, of space itself, "that I thought it would be nice to play."

"What do you mean play?" Malcolm asked while fear seemed to close his throat. He didn't want to know the answer. Because maybe he already knew it.

Martha reached her face down, so it was only inches from his own. Her eyes caught his and he realized that he did see something in their glassy exterior. He saw darkness. A shadow. Static.

She studied him for an eternity, and he did the same. Silence, the only companion.

She then smiled and spoke gently.

"With. My. Food."

Malcolm's whimpers turned to bloodcurdling screams as he felt himself get ripped apart by his hands. Hands and more hands reached their nails into his skin and pulled.

He felt like he was on fire as his skin was ripped from his body. And the worst thing was that he couldn't not watch.

No Martha held his head to watch as hand after bloodied hand reached out and tore off a new piece of him. Blood poured, gushed, and bubbled as they went deeper and deeper into his arms and legs.

Suddenly he felt a hand clasp his throat………

ABOUT THE AUTHOR

Britney Supernault

Britney Supernault, also known as the Cree Nomad, hails from the wintery north of Alberta, Canada. Coming from the small community of East Prairie Metis Settlement, Britney is proud of her Métis Cree background and settlement but is most often seen out of country.

An avid traveler, Cree Nomad is an experienced freelance writer, specializing in travel articles, but hopes to expand into the world of fiction by becoming an author herself. She hopes to publish her first novel in the next two years.

Having written and delivered over 120 articles this year alone, Britney prides herself as being 'the most determined writer you will ever meet'. Working mainly through the freelancing platforms Fiverr and Upwork, you can find the Cree Nomad seated at a café in some faraway country with a coffee in hand and her eyes trained on her laptop.

You can read more of her work in her personal blog at Creenomad.com, or by visiting her Instagram page: Cree_Nomad.

If you'd like to hire her for any articles, blog posts, or your ghostwriting needs, feel free to contact her through her Fiverr or Upwork profiles, or email her at: thecreenomad@gmail.com.

DON'T SLEEP!

By Frederick Trinidad

"Doc, this time I really need to stay awake. Tonight, I'll die if I sleep." a patient announced with a pleading expression.

The nurse then turned to me with a worried look in her eyes. I understood her feelings towards the situation because I share the same anxiety.

Mikhail was an indigent homeless man who came to us a few days before, asking for Analeptic drugs to keep him awake.

He was afraid of sleep.

It wasn't a congenital condition, which means he wasn't born with the ailment. Only recently, he started to have fear of sleeping but he couldn't tell us why.

He was hyperactive when I first saw him, thus instead of uppers, I suggested downer drugs in order to help him sleep. But he wouldn't take it and insisted I give him stimulants.

He practically begged for the drugs that will keep him awake.

He didn't have symptoms of drug dependency or being an addict so his actions puzzled me. He seemed to have the proper characteristics of being Somniphobic or having the fear of sleep and staying asleep.

So, I did what I could to help him.

I yielded to prescribing him the stimulants but insisted that he go see a mental health professional for proper diagnosis and treatment. I could refer him to a good specialist but being a destitute fellow, I knew he wouldn't be able to afford it.

I'm just a general practitioner in a government-run, 12-hour free clinic located in the poor side of town, with a single nurse as my assistant.

We wish we could improve the clinic's health care facilities for our poverty-stricken patients but there's only so much we could do. The reason why we're so worried is that we've had 6 sleep deaths since the previous week and Mikhail was displaying the same symptoms.

All the previous patients inexplicably died in their sleep.

I could barely put the pieces together but one thing is for sure, their fear of sleep is closely associated with fear of dying.

Yes, Somniphobia is a relatively common ailment and many adults, including myself, experience this at some point in their lives. But as a mental health issue, it should stay that way; a psychosis. Meaning; they shouldn't actually die.

In the medical world, there is something called SUDS or sudden unexpected/unexplained death syndrome.

The cause of death range from heart failures, sleep apnea, and many other anxiety-related disorders but to have them happen in a concentrated area in rapid succession is wildly puzzling to me.

And with Mikhail and those other patients, I am left bewildered as to what's going on. Besides the usual advice and prescription, there's nothing more I could do for him.

The next day, we received news of Mikhail's death.

He was found sprawled across a gutter with his face buried in the shallow water. Save for the minor wound on his forehead as a result of falling, the coroner found no signs of foul play.

The dirt on the backside of his pants suggested he was in a seated position before falling to his death.

"The wound on his forehead shows no clotting; it didn't start to heal at all." The coroner revealed when I paid him a visit in the aftermath of Mikhail's death.

"He's already dead before hitting the ground" I concluded to which the coroner agreed upon.

Unlike the two others, who were found lying peacefully on their usual resting spots on the pavement; Mikhail appeared to be seated and must've accidentally fallen asleep before dying.

"He's the 7th this month, all homeless bums. But we shouldn't be impressed by eerie coincidences, right Doc?" The coroner implied to which I reluctantly nodded upon.

I went to the clinic for my shift that evening and shared everything I learned with Mary, my nurse. Once again, she tried to convince me to report the anomaly to medical authorities. But the situations are still far too few and circumstantial to be escalated as a valid national concern.

We decided to sit tight for now and hope there would no longer be such incidents. But only later that evening, another patient with similar concerns walks in. This time, we would learn a bit more about what's been happening.

Steve was only in his early 30's but he looked like he's already in his 50's. The wrinkles on his face, his disheveled clothes, and the bold patches of hair upon his head revealed the extreme stress he's been going through.

And like Mikhail, he's afraid of sleeping.

To our luck, he is one of those very few individuals who were able to retain vivid memories of their dreams.

"It's a shadow. At first, it started appearing from a distance. But then, it gradually moved closer and closer each time I sleep." Steve confided in us.

Mary and I listened closely to what he had to say. We could no longer dismiss the issue as mere figments of imagination. As we now have 7 deaths in our hands, we could no longer ignore a possible epidemic that hunts victims in their sleep.

"I know that the next time the shadow appears, he'll definitely kill me" Steve spoke with trembling words.

"Just a shadow? Or, could it look like a shadow of someone you might know?" I queried intending to expound on his thoughts.

I was not expecting a concise answer rather; my questions were designed to make the subject explore his thoughts on a deeper level.

Steve paused for a while staring into nothingness, then his eyes widened as he arrived at a substantial realization.

"Harry…" Steve whispered.

His face turned pale and a look of extreme horror filled his eyes.

"It's Harry... I gotta get outta here." Steve turned to us while speaking in a slightly louder voice. He then dashed for the door and scrambled out of the building.

Mary and I looked at each other, stupefied as to what just happened.

The next day, I went over to a known area where the homeless usually lodges on. Amidst the rusty steel drums, makeshift tents, and all sorts of rubbish, I fruitlessly asked the dwellers of Steve's whereabouts.

Then, a curious thought came over my mind.

I started asking about "Harry."

That's when everyone widened their gaze upon me then proceeded to avoid talking to me altogether. I then knew there was something amiss and those people know a lot more than they're letting on.

I went to work that afternoon to start our evening shift, confident that my inquiries shall soon uncover the mystery. And maybe, hopefully, put a stop to these constant deaths. As always, I shared my findings with Mary and went about our patient care jobs.

That evening, one of the patients approached me with a stunning revelation.

"Doc, you were asking around about Harry, right?" The young homeless woman asked me.

"Yes. Do you know him?" I asked.

She looked around with weary eyes, seemingly worried for her safety. I assured her that the information won't tie back to her.

"Harry won 30 thousand dollars in the lottery. Or so we thought... " Her voice shook as she started telling the story.

She then buried her face in her palms and started sobbing inconsolably.

"We didn't mean for him to die, the plan was to rough him up a bit till he agrees to share the winnings." The young lady confessed.

The story goes, is that Harry announced to the entire community that he has a 30k dollar winning ticket.

He went around announcing he'll cash in the winnings, treat everyone to a night filled with food and drinks, and leave for his hometown soon after.

The community had other ideas and ended up beating Harry to death when he refused to equally share the winnings among them.

But as soon as they went to the Lottery District office to make the claim, they discovered that Harry mistook one of the winning numbers in the ticket.

He was one number short of winning 30 thousand dollars.

The ticket did win a hundred dollars to which the community shared among themselves.

The young lady didn't participate in the beating nor did she accept her portion of the $100 winning. But she admitted to not doing anything to stop the murder nor did she do anything to prevent the cover-up.

Harry's dead body was carried off to a nearby park and buried in a shallow grave. His death was never reported to the authorities and no one ever turned up looking for him.

Thus, it was as though he never existed.

I gave the lady some calming medicine, a few dollars for food, and send her on her way. Mary and I agreed to report the incident to the police the following day.

As sad and as revealing the young woman's story may be, it still doesn't explain the succession of sleep deaths happening in the area.

"So apparently, this 'Harry' haunts those people in their sleep" Mary stated to which both she and I inconclusively retired to.

At the same time, I couldn't help but feel very sad for this Harry character.

Nevertheless, I went home that evening knowing that we're many steps closer to unraveling the mystery.

For the first time in a while, I had a good night's sleep.

After many hours of peaceful slumber, I woke up to the alarming comprehension that I was running late for work. I stepped into the clinic to find a few patients already waiting to be examined.

"Sorry, I'm late." I apologized to Mary.

"It's okay. By the way, I already dropped by the police station to file the report... They said they'll look into it." She flatly informed me.

"That's it? Seriously?" I asked, appalled by the police's apparent lack of interest.

"It's hardly surprising, Doc" Mary remarked as we both knew that blatant discrimination and total lack of concern towards the poor has been the norm in that god-forsaken city.

As proof, the very clinic where we work was put up as part of the government's appeasement program.

We make do with the second-rate facility we have, the low-class medical equipment and supplies, and the so-called funding only covered the bare minimum. Brushing off the annoyance aside, I steadily went about my work.

By the end of the night, I wrapped things up and told Mary I'll be dropping by the police station to file my own report before heading home.

"Hey, why bother yourself with it? I already filed the report." Mary said trying to convince me it's just a waste of time.

"No, I'll also light a fire under their asses!" I announced, expressing that I'll demand satisfaction from the authorities.

I quickly gathered my things to head out the door but Mary forcibly blocked my way.

"No, don't go!" Mary screamed paired with a horrendous look in her eyes. Something that I've never seen from her before.

"What's going on Mary?" I asked, completely baffled by her insistence. Offering no answer, she remained fixed upon the door.

"Wait, don't tell me..." I started to realize but struggled to let out the words.

"You... You never went to the police, did you? Do-do you have anything to do with those de-deaths?" I asked, mumbling words I was able to muster. Subtly shaking her head was the only reaction she offered.

For a moment, all the conversations and all the interactions I ever had with her came crashing down on me. I could not believe the killer has always been right under my nose.

Intending to give her a false sense of security, I slouched by the edge of a table. Catching her by surprise, I suddenly bolted towards her, and then forcefully shoved her off the door.

I descended the grueling steps of the indoor stairs to finally reach the exit. I stepped out in the open when a blunt, heavy object fell on my head.

Everything went black.

I woke up with an intense pain lingering on the backside of my head. I opened my eyes to see Mary seating right across from me, we were back in the clinic.

"I'm sorry love, I had to do it... " She started explaining.

"No, you did alright my love." I interrupted her.

I stretched my body in order to regain my balance.

"How long has it been since I took em'?" I asked her.

"About 3 days since, my love." She replied.

I poured wine in two of the glasses on the table while I recall everything that we've been doing.

"We've only gotten 7, there's still a whole bunch of them left to kill." She stated with excitement building in her voice.

She then moved across the room towards the medicine cabinet. She pulled out a plethora of hallucinogenic drugs including LSD, mescaline, psilocybin, and PCP.

"Ready for another round?" Mary asked with a smile.

"You know what, I don't need them anymore..."

"This time, I want to kill them myself." I declared.

Mary smiled and looks a lot happier with my choice.

"For Harry!" we both exclaimed as we raised our glasses to a toast.

You see, Harry was my estranged, destitute brother who lived in the streets. Despite barely having enough for himself, he gave what little he could to help with my medical studies.

He later got incarcerated for thievery and we gradually lost contact. I started working in a government-owned clinic within the city and I never heard from him again.

One fine day, a patient visited our clinic to receive a consultation. Weighed down with so much grief, he fully confessed his crime after imposing patient-doctor confidentiality, not knowing that it was their victim's brother he was confessing to.

He became Somniphobic as a result of the guilt from killing my dear brother.

Yes, he felt guilty.

But not guilty enough to turn himself in, along with his partners in crime. I exacted revenge by slowly poisoning him with high doses of analeptic drugs.

But I was held down by guilt the moment he died.

Still, my heart was filled with so much wrath that I was willing to do anything to destroy those who have taken my brother's life. And my nurse Mary, who has fallen deeply in love with me, decided to assist me on my quest for vengeance.

We decided that I should take high doses of hallucinogens so that I could continue killing mindlessly and mercilessly.

From then on, I've been purposely giving and prescribing those bastards with enough doses of upper drugs in order to kill them slowly.

As their intake of the stimulants increased, so did their guilt and paranoia. The drugs accelerated Harry's appearance within their dreams. By doing so, Harry and I worked together towards the same goal.

In a way, by killing those murdering fools, I grew ever closer to my brother. The lack of proper rest would inevitably kill them during their most vulnerable moment.

Death would always take them while they're asleep.

Taking full advantage of the city's discrimination towards the poor, I knew the coroner would never properly examine their bodies for traces of drugs.

Mary and I came up with the perfect concoction of hallucinogenic drugs that I should take.

The psychotic drugs were so powerful that I'd forget my crimes up to a point, and then I'll have to take the drugs again.

At times, I would even totally forget about Harry.

But no longer.

This time, I want to exterminate these criminals with exacting clarity.

The next day greeted my beloved Mary and me with several new patients from the same homeless community.

They were suffering from Somniphobia.

We cheerfully welcomed them into our clinic.

ABOUT THE AUTHOR
Frederick Trinidad

Frederick has been in the business of ghostwriting for a couple of years now. He wrote blogs for brands, web articles, social media posts, and scripts for different YouTube channels.

However, writing stories has been his passion since childhood and this anthology is his way of expanding his writing career and reaching a wide range of audiences. He discovered his love for horror storytelling during the peak of the pandemic when the world held its breath amidst a global state of uncertainty.

His innovative style of writing is designed to make readers experience his distinctive brand of horror and mystery for themselves.

Fred wrote a mystery/thriller novel that he works to see published by the first quarter of 2022. The short story contributions that he imparted in this anthology shall give you a peek at the horror that awaits you in that book and his literary works in the future.

To receive updates from his work, you can follow his personal Facebook account at:
https://www.facebook.com/frederick.trinidad.3

You can also reach him via email at: trinidadfred79@gmail.com

SINISTER

By Chemsou Khodja

The icy air stung his lungs and the rocky mud path slowed his movement and yet he kept on climbing the Appalachian mountain.

This was nothing but a seasonal escape from the mundane and routine, from technology and, above all, the pressures of his work. Working in a psych ward takes its toll on the human mind and his was no different.

He would go camp in unknown spots of nature and cleanse his soul from the ghosts of the sick and deranged. He had parked his car at a gas station parking lot at the base of the mountain and chatted with a group of hikers much like himself; One girl he particularly liked. Then set off on foot for his journey.

On his back, he carried a bag with provisions, a backpacking tent and a pocket knife for protection. In his pocket, a lighter. He had left his cell phone in the car and alerted no one of his departure, for he would only be away a couple of days and he had been on so many trips before while nothing alarming happened. He had no reason to think that would change.

It was almost noon, and he stopped to eat cold rice and chicken he brought with him. There, sat on a rock, he listened to the wind strum the snowy trees of the land like a choir of nature. The sound almost gloomy with the grey skies and absent sun.

He had reached enough altitude to see the shapes of the white mountains stretching to the horizon and rising to the dark clouds like tombstones for dead giants, and it was in this raw wilderness which inhabited no man but him, he felt the most alive.

On his way up, he encountered a wild hare with blood on his fur. At first look it seemed as if the animal was hurt and on the run from a predator, but after much observation he saw there was no scratch on the thing and that the blood was not the rabbit's.

The afternoon came with howling winds and snowing skies and the path he treaded through was coated in white. He cursed at the unexpected change in the weather as he rubbed his arms for warmth.

He had surveyed the weather forecast the whole week and nothing told of an upcoming storm. Only an hour later and his vision was a white grainy canvas, his hat and gloves wet with melted snow. He had lost the mountain trail and so he prodded through the unknown forest. Setting the tent would not work, for the wind would undoubtedly tear it up. With his arms tight around him, he walked on, forming a trail in the deep snow.

He had been shivering when he reached a clearing in the forest; a white carpet of foamy snow. In the middle was a structure a little bigger than a shack. He had no choice but to see if he could get in, assuming no one lived there, which he was almost sure of.

The old metallic door swung open with ease and he noticed the locks on the inside. The room, if he could call it that, was cold and dirty and smelled like rotten meat so badly that it burned his throat, and the walls had animal skins and limbs pinned to them.

On the ground was a set of scattered bones of which he did not know the origin, and the sight of them gave him a crushing sense of uneasiness and dread. The kitchen counter on his left had glass jars. Some that were filled with herbs and oils and some with worms and hair and some he could never imagine.

The place had no windows and only a fireplace with cold but new coal. He knew then this place was not abandoned and that someone, yet where they were, was what worried him. All he cared about now was that he was not freezing to death in the storm outside.

At the corner of the room was a trap that he opened and found it lead downstairs. A ladder that seemed to stretch down to the dark depths of the earth. Filled with curiosity, he grabbed his torch from his pack and climbed down. His body senses were sending him all the grim signals, but he had to know what kind of place this was.

He touched solid ground after few steps, and the room seemed to be a cellar of some sorts, with cupboards and shelves. The smell was even stronger here, and the air had a particular heaviness to it.

Pitch black was the room except for the blaring projection of his torch, swinging about. He stopped at a spot on the wall and his heart sank to his knees. An old woman's face, blackened and wrinkly, skinned and pinned with nails. Her eyes a dark endless void that watched him and her lips gaping in a scream.

Around it were amulets and bones that formed the shape of a pentagram. Below on the ground, a bucketful of bowels and guts and god knows what, and he retched at the sight of it.

It was clear to him and anyone with a normal view on life that whoever inhabited here was no more than a sinister creature one must not cross paths with.

He was disturbed for a man who practically worked in an asylum and thought of ditching this godforsaken house and trying his luck with the storm until he heard the door creak open and heavy footsteps thumped above.

He cursed under his breath and turned off his flashlight. Panicking, he hid behind one cupboard in the farthest corner from the ladder, forgetting his backpack behind. It was too late to get it, for the footsteps were coming down the ladder.

In the dimness, he peeked from behind the cupboard, a figure so tall and large it seemed more bear than man. He stood there facing the face on the wall, his breathing loud and inconsistent.

"Hey ma. I bring you somethin pretty." The man said in a voice so repugnant and ungodly to the ear it sounded like the grating of metal.

He crouched and put something on the ground. It took a moment for his eyes to adjust to the darkness, but when he saw, he did his best not to vomit. Decapitated and mutilated was the head of the girl he had talked to that morning. And the world around seemed to spin, and he held himself to not fall.

"Anythin for you, ma. What? dad's always happy with what I bring him, why not you? I don't care about their bodies, I just need their heads. What? Fuck you. Today's good. I bring you more gifts, promise. I have to go make dinner now." He talked to the lifeless face as if it conversed with him.

The man moved back to the ladder but stopped and turned towards the darkness he hid in. Standing like a giant shadow, unmoving for a moment.

"Is someone here, ma? Why didn't you tell me?" He said while pointing to the backpack, "Liar! Then what's that, huh? What's that?"

He grabbed the camping backpack and felt it with his hands, as if he had seen nothing like it.

"I know you're in the cupboard. Ma told me."

His blood froze.

The savage walked to the cupboard and opened its door. Even behind it, he could smell the rotting stench of sweat and other smells he could not name and he held his breath, fearing his heartbeats would alert the man from behind the furniture.

"He's not here, ma! I go look outside." The man strode to the upper floor with the backpack.

He knew this was his chance to get out of there and he sneaked to the wall and slowly climbed it when he heard the man step out of the house. Behind him, he felt the skinned face watching him with hollow pits as eyes and it made his skin crawl.

He reached the door and peeked outside for a way to escape to the forest. What he found instead was the freak looking at him from yards away, grinning.

In the story of the three little pigs and the wolf, each had hid in his house and the wolf came and destroyed all he could. But it said nothing about hiding in the wolf's den itself.

That was what he had done as he sat in the middle of the room, hands cupped over ears as the freak slammed with all his might at the metal door, whirling particles of dust. He had expected the door to come down tumbling and whatever massacre would come next, but to his luck; it stood solid.

He remembered his face clearly when he saw him; an ugly, deformed mouth and nose and eyes that projected pure evil. Scars that sculpted his skin. Limbs lacking proper proportion that radiated violence.

The knocking had stopped and the inbred degenerate had taken to circling the shack and hitting at the wooden walls, peering between the slits at him like a cat with a birdcage.

"Ma's gonna be happy, so happy. She loves guests. She has one now, go join them. Let me in, let me show you to ma, let me in!"

He said as he clawed the wood.

He sat on the ground shaking and hugging his knees and felt like the room was getting smaller and the walls closed in on him each minute. What the freak did dwarfed anything he had ever seen in patients at the asylum. He finally built enough courage to tell the degenerate to stay away from him, but that only agitated him more.

"I'm gonna fucking kill you, hear me? Hear me? Look, I have your stuff. You want them? Let me in. I need to show you ma. I promised. I promised!" He wailed at the top of his lungs.

Sunset was near, and the circus had diminished but not completely stopped. The freak was still persistent. A little while later, the storm was back, and the freak ceased his hunt. The last he heard from him was:

"I'll come back, ma! You take good care of our guest."

He spent the night hungry and cold, forcing himself to stay awake and think of a way to escape. The storm outside was too violent to make a run for it and he expected the degenerate to know that.

He felt a disturbing presence on him, a chill of death and evil radiating from the basement. That was enough for him to know what to do. It seemed insane, but the whole situation was, and the life he led was changed forever.

He grabbed the oil jars and old cheap whiskeys and beers and poured them all over the room. What remained he poured down the trap and again, he felt a presence disturbing his soul, coming from the face in the wall. He sat on the only dryspot and pulled his lighter from his pocket and verified it still worked.

Morning came and the moment of truth came with it. The storm had died down, and the degenerate was nowhere to be seen. He built enough momentum, and he opened the door wide open. The foamy new snow stood between him and the white forest. He turned, lit his lighter, threw it at the open trap and set off running as he heard flames forming.

When he reached the treeline, a trunk of an arm slammed him to the ground, knocking the breath out of him. The freak grabbed at this throat and his weight crushed him. Amidst the struggle, the degenerate planted the pocketknife in his chest and stood above him.

"What did you do to ma?" the freak screamed as he ran towards the flaming cabin and without hesitation entered it.

He struggled to turn his head and see, and the blood was oozing out of his chest and mouth. After seconds, he heard the wailings of the burning monstrosity and he pushed himself against a tree and watched with a blurry vision the structure burn.

The flames dancing to the sky. The walls as they fell apart, formed two holes in the shack as if hell had eyes, and he found it eerily resembled the face in the wall.

ABOUT THE AUTHOR
Chemsou Khodja

Chemsou Khodja is a young aspiring author with a burning passion for all aspects of storytelling. Broadcasting his ever-developing skills through different disciplines and genres ranging from sci-fi, horror to thrillers and so on.

He works partly on upwork as a fiction writer and has created multiple stories for multiple clients.

The one you've read is a horror short story. One that is filled with suspense and hopefully, gritty bone-chilling writing. Enjoy.

To see his portfolio and services, visit his upwork profile: https://www.upwork.com/freelancers/~01124ee37a9213363d

CARRIED AWAY

By Manuel Bocchia

click-click-click

The room reeked of confinement and loneliness. The one window that could allow a little air in stood shut, as it seemed it had remained for a long time.

clack-clack-clack

Laundry, wrappings, and stained food trays piled up in every corner of the room, concealed by a dull darkness. The posters on the walls were barely noticeable under the strobing lights emitted by the monitor screen in the center of the space.

Click-clack-clickity-clacks sounds from the keyboard and mouse filled the room, along with the deafening noise of the tiny fans inside the computer case which stood on the desktop. Hundreds of tiny lights danced away from the see-through plastic of the computer, forging patterns that created a particularly illusory atmosphere.

Pete sat in front of his computer, focused and unhinged, frantically clicking and shouting at his monitor. The match had been bitterly contested due to his teammates - he had let them know as much. His nine kills and zero deaths obviously vouched for his performance. The rest of his team – well, they didn't even seem to be trying. They were giving away kills and losing ground, they weren't securing objectives, and didn't care to communicate at all.

Just as well, thought Pete, I can do all the communication myself. He noticed every little mistake and made sure everyone on the team was aware of it. It was his responsibility after all: there was no doubt he was the best player in this match – and every match, since at least a couple of months ago. It just seemed that the matchmaking system wasn't going to award him with a good team anytime soon.

Pete figured he was just too good and, with a good team, he'd be unstoppable. He was aware that video game companies had different techniques for finding balance in their games, and he had no problem suffering low-skill teammates in general, but this last streak had been horrible. No amount of shouting and correcting seemed to do anything for his awful allies – they all sucked.

Pete brought his best – as he always did – and still, they lost. Bitter end. More curses, some strong, personal messages, and a couple of reported players later, Pete quit the game, took a sip of soda from his cup, and looked at the time.

As fluid entered his body, he realized he hadn't let any of it out for a while – except, of course, a handful of spit and sweat drops. Pete removed his headphones and headed down the hall.

Unburdened, he came back under the lights of his realm. On and off, red, green, blue, every color of the rainbow flashed and danced, perhaps a pretend club. Behind his computer desk and his extremely stylish and comfortable office chair, there was the window. Phone in hand, he approached it as he wandered around the room, gaining back feeling on his legs.

He inspected the news headlines, saved a couple to later read in full – the commentary section, of course:

"New Zombie franchise collapses after poor reception: Zack Snyder on the ropes", *"The ten truths behind Roswell you need to know NOW"*, and *"Security Breach: every detail on the epic fail of browser updates."*

He'd share some strong opinions on each topic before dinner, but first, he had to go over every little detail of his defeat to save a record of his teammates' awful gameplay, create a video gallery, and share it all over social media. A few likes, shares, and comments were poor substitution to the pleasure of victory, but at least it soothed his rage somewhat.

dot-dot-dot

There were sudden, muffled noises. Small things hitting the window next to his ear. He turned off his phone screen and glanced outside. A sudden gust of wind blew sand, twigs, and leaves to the pane, jumping Pete.

It was dark outside; with the storm, even darker. The gale had picked up after the dark clouds had gathered in the sky. It was definitely going to rain soon – perhaps even a bit of hail. You never knew about that.

He saw the people shuffling down the street, moving their cars around, parking under trees, and rushing to their homes to save their vehicles from the ice. It was all the same to him, he had no way – and no need, really – to move around. The availability of delivery services and online banking made his introverted paradise a reality.

He closed the dark drapes and turned his back on the world. Sitting again in front of his digital desktop, he went back to business. Right back to where he left off. Back again at it.

Capturing, editing, composing, Pete produced the most marvelous cases against terrible teams. It was all a problem of the matchmaking system in his mind, but you can't go against big corporations; it's much easier to go against the little guy.

Sometimes you'd get a reply or two from them, some were hurt, some even angry, and that's all Pete wanted. A reaction. For them to take credit. And for him, recognition for good gameplay.

He was lucky to be able to dedicate a lot of his time to playing this seriously in this particular game. This wasn't just a hobby for him, so he should play only with those on his same mindset, otherwise… these things happened, he thought as he went through every minute detail, in every minute of the game, detecting validating footage.

A good few hours later, Pete was booting up, once again, his favorite game. He had blown off some steam with all those posts and comments and was ready for a rematch.

blip

A sudden error. Internet was gone, it seemed. Can't play multiplayer with no connection. He checked the settings.

blip

More errors. No luck, restarting the adapter from the PC wasn't helping, not even reconnecting the line with the router.

Lamenting himself, Pete headed towards the router to pull all the plugs and wait a bit for it to go back to normal. As he waited, he checked his social media. He went through his chat groups, sending stickers and GIFs away for a bit while thunder rolled and rain erupted outside

ting

He got mail. The sender wasn't familiar to him, but the message was flagged as important. Pete hoped it wasn't about work.

There was no subject, and he was surprised to see a single line of text inside the body of the e-mail.

From: 17956275@duckmail.com

To: pete.master.64@coolmail.com

Are you content with your actions?

Pete was stunned after reading the message. What was this SPAM? There was no link to click, no images nor a Nigerian prince.

Just a six-letter-long question. *'Am I content with my actions?'* he thought, not really understanding the question. *'What is this supposed to mean? Who the hell does this?'*

The username was indeed unrecognizable: a meaningless string of numbers. He performed a quick search but the numbers did indeed seem to be random. *'This is some strange shit indeed,'* he reflected.

Pete deleted the message and plugged the router back in. He was headed back to the toilet when…

ting

'What now?'

Perhaps it was a coupon for a delivery or some new stories from friends? He checked his phone without paying too much attention to that murmuring in the back of his mind, especially after it seemed he had gotten another e-mail in his inbox. He was fast to tap on it.

From: 17956275@duckmail.com

To: pete.master.64@coolmail.com

Will you not answer my question?

He was at a loss. There was no unsubscribe button. It started to seem to him that this wasn't SPAM; someone was writing this to him. Perhaps some sort of automated script? Why would it target him? There weren't many platforms that had access to his personal e-mail account. What was going on?

Pete sat at his desk as he deleted the new mail, and started furiously typing at the keyboard.

blip

Everything was offline. Restarting the router didn't do the trick. It seemed the problem wasn't local, and he was locked out from the web for now. Luckily his phone still had data.

ting

A chill ran up his spine as he heard the ringtone and felt the vibration in his pocket. Slowly, he woke his phone in his hand and confirmed his suspicion. Another e-mail, same sender.

From: 17956275@duckmail.com

To: pete.master.64@coolmail.com

This is not a game, Peter. Stop ignoring me or you will stay offline forever.

Something was terribly wrong.

Panic was starting to settle in his guts. The message was blurred as his hand trembled slightly in place. *'What the hell is this?'*

Involuntarily, he touched the reply button and scrambled to put a coherent idea together.

From: pete.master.64@coolmail.com

To: 17956275@duckmail.com

Who are you? What do you want?

The message was sent as Pete's heart pounded his chest. It seemed his solar plexus wouldn't hold it together for much longer.

ting

The reply could've been an instant message; the unknown sender was a terribly fast writer.

From: 17956275@duckmail.com

To: pete.master.64@coolmail.com

There you are. Welcome to the conversation, Peter.

It doesn't matter much who I am or what I want, dear Peter.

It's more about what I can do for you.

But let me go back to the beginning because you still haven't answered my initial inquiry.

Are you content?

Pete's head rushed uncontrollably. Even though the wind and rain had gotten worse in the last few seconds, the boiling noise in his ears was unmatched by the racket outside.

He replied slowly again.

From: pete.master.64@coolmail.com

To: 17956275@duckmail.com

I have no idea what you are talking about. Please leave me alone.

Soon enough, a reply.

From: 17956275@duckmail.com

To: pete.master.64@coolmail.com

Peter, you have no idea the power I have over you. You are in no position of demanding anything. I'm asking you a simple question, and I require a swift answer. Otherwise, you'll have to learn the full scope of the situation.

"This is fucked up", concluded Pete. *"I won't continue indulging this asshole."*

From: pete.master.64@coolmail.com

To: 17956275@duckmail.com

Go fuck yourself.

Pete locked his phone screen and left the device on the desktop. He walked away from it, still under shock. He convinced himself that this was just a twisted fuck who liked playing games with random strangers. Having access to a semi-private address isn't difficult, especially in this day and age, and if he got his e-mail address, it was obvious he'd get his name as well. There was nothing to worry about.

ting

Pete launched himself on his phone with deranged ferocity.

From: 17956275@duckmail.com

To: pete.master.64@coolmail.com

Are you sure about that?

3 Files Attached: 121566666125.jpg, 121566666126.jpg, screen_caps.jpg

The pictures taunted him, menacing, waiting to be opened. He didn't dare do it. He was paralyzed.

After what felt like centuries, he opened the first one.

Cursing the storm which was striking his office window, cursing his luck for landing him in that situation, and especially cursing his network service provider because the picture was loading as if it were the nineties, his heart sunk when the picture finally opened.

It was a street-level picture of a very dark and stormy sky in the background, and in the foreground, there was the very familiar worn-out facade of his house. In the center of the picture: himself, phone in hand, leaning on his second-floor window not twenty minutes ago.

While he was unable to consciously move a muscle, his body couldn't help but automatically open the second picture, perhaps in the hope of removing such horrific sight from his phone.

On the contrary, the second picture was somehow worse; it showed his house internet line cable severed, and a pair of large scissors lying on the ground next to the vandalization. And next to the scissors, there were a couple of red gasoline drums and a large pile of rocks.

A third picture awaited. He was positively paralyzed from action, unable to grasp the situation. The storm roared outside; wind and rain were incessant, and now hail too was beating his house with no remorse. Still numb, his thumb pressed the final photo.

A large collection of screenshots filled his phone screen. Dozens of posts, comments, and messages collaged on the image he had to pinch in to identify. He did, indeed, identify them; they were all his.

His comments. His posts. His messages. Curses, expositions, rants: all were evident in that file. It shocked him to see them all gathered here: a reflection of hatred and impulsiveness.

ting

He pressed on the new message.

From: 17956275@duckmail.com

To: pete.master.64@coolmail.com

Are you content with your actions?

Pete was astounded. He knew not what to do or say. He'd never been put in a place like this. Still caught in a brain lapse, not capable of thinking straight or elaborating further, he replied as he could.

From: pete.master.64@coolmail.com

To: 17956275@duckmail.com

No please I'm sorry

He didn't dare move close to the window to check. Supporting himself by the threshold, lightheaded but still panicking, he watched the entrance from afar.

CRASH

A large rock had broken through the glass, and the sound of the storm erupted in the room. Rain and hail were cascading under the blowing curtains, and outside there was lightning.

A silhouette of a man got projected through the opening, and it was clearly visible as he enlarged the window hole with his feet and tossed the red drums inside which poured liters of nauseating liquid over the floor.

The pool of gasoline engulfed his feet as he was sat on the floor, frozen still in the doorway, his eyes fixed on the assaulter in front of him.

The dark hooded figure was now peering through the broken window and the unsteady curtains, unconcerned by the large hail now falling from the sky impacting his body.

And even though this was the loudest hail storm in history, the figure's voice was heard crystal clear in that room as he lit his lighter and flung it inside.

"Too late for sorry, you toxic monster."

And Pete's world was devoured by flame.

ABOUT THE AUTHOR
Manuel Bocchia

Manuel Bocchia is an amateur musician, artist, and writer from Argentina, where he works professionally as an English teacher.

Bilingual to the bone, Manuel keeps a blog in both Spanish and English in which he occasionally reviews films, shares his thoughts, and tells a few stories.

His favorite genres are fantasy, thriller and magical realism. He has also written plays, and scripts for YouTube and animation.

Manu also plays piano, guitar, bass and ukulele, sings with a rich baritone voice, and especially adores indie, lofi and chiptunes. He has recorded two solo, homemade albums as manumanu which can be streamed in YouTube.

When he isn't teaching, writing, singing or reading, he spends some time drawing and painting to relax, or studying philosophy and programming to become a better person, or even perhaps change careers.

You can find more about Manuel Bocchia through Instagram @manu.bocchia or Twitter @manu_bocchia.

BUZZ

By Oktay Ibrahimov

Ozzy drove into town at noon. A few business meetings later, he was free to explore, which as usual ended with him looking for a hotel that was a tad more respectable than a motel but not as expensive as a real hotel.

The town itself was the usual midwestern American sleepy collection of houses, only given any sort of industry to appeal to folks like Ozzy. People who pass by and only stay with the excuse of seeing that one landmark that would really only consume 5 minutes of their time, but serves well enough as a reason to spend the night in a comfy bed.

"When the clock strikes eight, you turn the lights off," the man behind the reception desk said absentmindedly, sifting through paperwork, "I recommend seven-thirty."

Ozzy remembered the words, even as he laid on his bed, watching the game on the big screen on the wall. He thought the clerk to be some weirdo, or maybe just so tired that he was spewing nonsense at the job.

He was very wrong. There was a strange thing about this town, something to do with turning the lights off before it was dark outside. And not just light, anything that emitted it too. That was what the clerk said. Him, others too.

The driver mentioned how it was not always at eight. Just before the sun sets. There was a billboard just before the sign that welcomed visitors in. An old one, dirty with dust, half of it unreadable.

Ozzy could make it out though, although he did not pay any attention to it at the time. The clerk's advice to him triggered the memory. The billboard displayed a moth on a light bulb, the moth lit up with the light bulb, and when both were off, 'Lights off by sundown' lit up instead. Well, the 't' and the 'y' and the 'o's did not, but anybody could deduce the meaning. "This fucking country has the weirdest people, I swear..."

His eyes wandered around the room as he thought about the town's strange policy. Maybe they did it to save money on electricity or something. The room he stayed in was not exactly spacious, but it was certainly bigger than he expected.

The walls were bare, he could see the concrete, which was not exactly aesthetically pleasing, but he supposed it fit the price. The bed was not comfy either, he would still get a good night's sleep though, he slept in these kinds of beds all the time on the road. Ozzy used the shower once and it was surprisingly pleasant.

Hot water, fresh towels, clean floor tiles, and of course the most important factor, small bottles of shampoo to pocket for later. It was sort of a road-nature balance. You take the small bottles from the places that have them and use them at the ones that do not. In fact, all of the room was oddly squeaky clean.

Not odd enough to worry, although, why would one worry about cleanliness was beyond Ozzy. Nothing seemed out of the ordinary, but still, this little weird thing they had with light annoyed Ozzy.

Just then, he heard the clerk's voice again. This time not in his head, but rather in the speakers outside his room, slightly raspy and unclear, but he could make it out.

DEAR GUESTS, WE KINDLY ADVICE AND URGE YOU TO TURN OFF ANY SOURCE OF LIGHT. THANK YOU, AND HAVE A GOOD EVENING.

He first thought it was something that was a weird law enforced by a local sheriff a century ago. Probably something like pot. Nobody can *technically* do it, but everybody does it anyway. Well, the other way around for this.

Maybe the clerk and the driver just wanted to make sure he would not get into any trouble with the authorities. Ozzy focused back on the TV screen. It was off, even though the remote was on the shelf nearby. He walked over and tried turning it on himself.

Nothing. He batted away a moth that was circling the lamp by the screen. Noticed another flying out of the bathroom where the lights were off and towards the ceiling's bulbs. Then the lights in the room went off. "Seriously?"

He walked to the windows and checked his smart watch. 7:50. The sky was the color of a purple bruise. Everything outside was dark. He made eye contact with an elderly woman on a porch. She seemed calm enough, waved at him with a smile, and went inside.

The lights behind the opaque windows of her house dimmed to darkness. So did the windows of the neighboring houses, "What in the world…"

Ozzy shrugged, "Maybe they are saving energy. Backwater towns, fuck. Gonna have to talk to Mike about this," he laid down on the bed and opened the app of the channel on his phone.

Didn't need the TV to watch the game.

The sky went dark when the game reached halftime. He was texting with someone, or was trying to at least, when a moth landed on the screen with an annoying *zzzzt*.

Ozzy batted it off. Another one. And another. Soon, there was a slight white noise in the room, a very faint cacophony of buzzing.

There must have been a lot of them around, hitting the walls, the bed frame, hell, he felt a few on the fabric of his clothes as well.

"What the…" Ozzy could not finish the sentence. A moth the size of his whole phone screen landed on it. He feverishly dropped it and jumped up from the bed, feeling shivers of disgust run down his back. Foul.

"How do they even get that big?" He quickly made his way to the door, hearing and feeling a few crunches under his feet along the way, stumbling in the dark.

He stopped for a brief thought, moved his foot around, as if he was putting out a stump of a cigarette. It felt a little wet. Slippery, for sure. Ozzy hurried at a slightly faster pace, doing his damndest to ignore the cracking under his soles and focusing on putting his feet down firmly one at a time. To his utter regret, the handle did not budge.

Ozzy knocked. "Hello? Staff?" he knocked louder and sighed. He pulled his second phone out, the one he used for business calls. A nervous smile was on his face, as he thought about what he might see if he was to illuminate the room.

He reached for the handle again, but his hand caught a large wing that twitched and buzzed off momentarily. Were they everywhere already? How long until there were too many to move? He had to call. Someone in the lobby would surely pick up.

Ozzy's thumb slid to the power button on the side of the phone.

He hesitated for a moment, another, and then pressed it.

In the split second that the screen illuminated the immediate space in front of Ozzy, he saw something that could simply not be real.

Multiple piles of moths swarming over one another on the walls and the ceiling was horrendous enough. Their wings were moving and hitting each other's bodies, the walls were not even visible. Same horrendous sight for the ceiling.

Even more so for the bulbs and the lamp, whole spheres of them coalesced together around the former sources of light, buzzing with greed to get deeper towards the glass in hopes of sensing light. There was a bigger one right in front of him. He could see a pair of segmented eyes, they were as big as his head.

Ozzy could see his own reflection in them for the breath that the space was lit up. A man grimacing with fear, disgust, repulsiveness, and emotions that he could not even describe. Something, some appendage of the creature in front of him batted the phone away.

Ozzy watched the phone's pale blue luminescence get consumed by the buzzing darkness the second it left his hand. He felt his heartbeat pick up. His hand pounded on the door, his fist producing crunches, rather than thuds. but he did not speak. He could barely breathe from fear.

Ozzy went to step away, thinking that moving to the window and attempting to escape from there could work. His foot met some resistance, as he felt little bodies fly off and fall down. Every step was followed by a louder crunch, he was walking on a carpet of dead insects.

Ozzy took a moment to take a breath, which served to be a horrible idea. A dozen moths got in his mouth, making him cough and retch, falling down on a knee, only to hear a louder crunch, close to the sound of his arm breaking when he was twelve.

The man pursed his lips. He would have to figure this out one way or another. Sprinting was his best bet, even though he was already tired. Ozzy was not in the best shape of his life, and even then, he made quick and short breaths, desperately trying to avoid getting any moths in his mouth or even nostrils.

He felt a bigger body land on his back. He could not make out how big, but he felt every movement of its leg. It crawled up to his shoulder and took off again, pushing Ozzy a tad forward. There was no way he could endure this anymore.

His skin was crawling, he felt like they were getting under his clothes. There was no way to tell whether he imagined it or not. There was no way to tell what laid ahead of him, or behind, or even above. He had to run.

Ozzy made a few quick deep breaths, making sure to cover his mouth so that no moths would get close. A few were batted away, although he felt his hand hit something meaty and fleshy.

He felt adrenaline rush through his body, prepared to take off. All he had to do was run and jump. The glass wouldn't hurt him. He would be fine. He had to be. That was the only way out.

Ozzy took a long, lunging, hopeful step forward. Another. And then rushed ahead, pushing off the floor and covering his head with his forearms, trying to place them in the way of the window. There was a crunch, as his body hit some number of bodies covering the window.

He rolled away, propelled by the moths flying off the window, the few of the bigger ones that survived the impact. His landing was quiet. The buzzing drowned out the crunches. Ozzy stood up, grimacing, cringing at the wetness on his soaking his back and his hands. He had to try again.

Ozzy took a step back, another and ran. He jumped, so close to the glass. A yelp of excitement was cut midway through a scream of pain.

"Your heartbeat is elevated."

The smart watch lit up.

A few hours later, the door clicked. A pair of people with masks and cleaning gear carefully stepped inside, taking in the scene. The floor was littered with a layer of dead moths of all sizes, some spots in the room seemed to be just dark green spots.

Some parts of the room were spotted with blood, there was a leg torn at the knee hanging over the broken TV screen. Broken bone was visible, as well as blood caked and still on hanging threads of sinew and muscle.

There was no other trace of Ozzy, safe for the phone on the ground by the door. The screen was cracked and the insides of it were spilled out. It looked ravished. The person nodded to the other one and the room was filled with the sound of a vacuum cleaner and the smell of bleach.

They had to prepare the room for the next guest.

ABOUT THE AUTHOR
Oktay Ibrahimov

OI I like writing. I like money. I like writing for money. Any and all genres are within my writing abilities, and I would highlight dialogue and characters as my strong suits, that is when the story calls for them.

Anyway, I don't have a lot to say about myself, but do hire me please, if you enjoyed the piece you read.

CHECK OUT THESE TITLES

Creepy Nightmares

Horror Stories To Tell In The Dark: Book 1, 2, 3, 4

Scary Short Stories For Teens: Book 1, 2 & 3

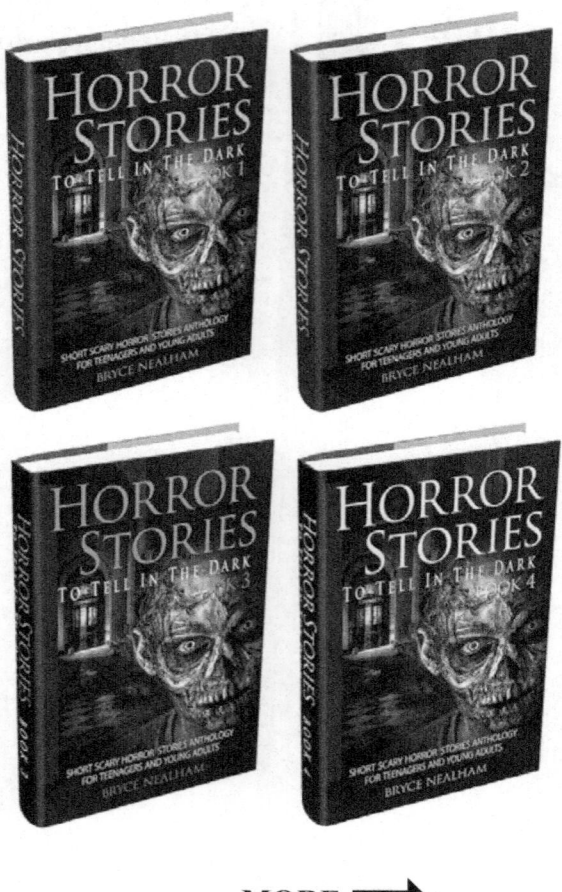

MORE ➡

MORE COMING SOON!